Fairy Dog HEAVEN

WRITTEN BY
PATRESE FISCHER

ILLUSTRATED BY
MARCUS CUTLER

For Noah and Ellie.
In loving memory of Molly,
our favorite fairy dog.

See if you can find Molly throughout this book!

A dog is a special gift from above sent down to show you unconditional love.

Our time with them is far too short and when that time has come to an end, it feels as if our broken hearts may never mend.

It is so very sad for us to see them go,
but this is a little secret about dogs you
should know.

When they leave this Earth,
our furry friends gain fairy
wings.

And spend their days in fairy dog heaven doing their favorite things.

In fairy dog heaven, sticks, balls and
frisbees sail through the air,
so fairy dogs can play fetch all day
without a care.

In fairy dog heaven, fairy dogs can dig
and dig and dig...

...and make holes that are really, really, really big.

In fairy dog heaven, there is a gigantic buffet so tasty and great - not a drop of kibble there, only chicken, steak, and juicy bones to fill up their plate.

And when fairy dogs get thirsty, there are millions of toilets where they can get a drink.

They can even choose whether or not they want it to stink!

In fairy dog heaven, fairy dogs can always
find something fun to chew -
a couch, a rug and even a shoe or two!

In fairy dog heaven, there are piles and piles of dirty clothes, great for diving into with a wet little nose.

In fairy dog heaven, a trip to go potty is as fun as can be...

TOP SCORES

1 MOLLY...450 987

2 TOBY...364 009

3 RUFUS 268 003

* * *

... when fairy dogs take aim at their favorite hydrant or tree.

20

50

100

In fairy dog heaven, deliveries come 100 times a day because there is nothing a fairy dog loves more than to chase and bark as packages make their way.

And when the night begins to fall, fairy dogs
do the most special thing of all.

With their owners fast asleep and tucked
under a sheet, fairy dogs fly down to
Earth to give them a big lick on their
face and sometimes even their feet!

So if you are feeling sad and missing
your very best friend...

...think of them in fairy dog heaven
doing their favorite things and visiting
you in your dreams at day's end.